All Ab...

Piglet

This book belongs to . . . .

Meet Piglet

Piglet may be a Very Small Animal, but he has a big heart. Known to be a tiny bit Anxious sometimes, he tries very hard with everything he does, especially when practising writing his own name:

Being small, Piglet likes to have Company. This often means holding Winnie-the-Pooh's paw (just to be sure of him), for Pooh is his very best friend.

In this book, you too can keep Piglet company and learn all about some of his Big Adventures (Big for one quite so Small).

In which we read about

Piglet

One sunny afternoon, when Piglet, Winnie-the-Pooh
and Christopher Robin were enjoying a friendly talk
together, Christopher Robin happened to say,

"Piglet, I saw a heffalump today".

Piglet felt a little uneasy, but wanted to sound as if he knew what Christopher Robin was talking about. "I saw one once," he replied. "At least, I think I did."

By and by, Piglet and Pooh decided it was time to go home and walked side-by-side through the Forest.

After a moment, Pooh said solemnly, "Piglet, I have decided something."

"What's that, Pooh?"

"I have decided to catch a heffalump,"

he declared.

Piglet said nothing, but only because he rather wished *he* had come up with the idea first.

However, soon he had forgotten his disappointment and set about helping Pooh work out how to trap a heffalump. It seemed that digging a Very Deep Pit would be a good start; a deep pit very near a heffalump so that the heffalump might fall into it quite quickly. Pooh and Piglet then wondered how one might keep the heffalump there once trapped . . .

"Supposing you wanted to catch *me*," pondered Pooh, "how would *you* go about it?"

Piglet thought for a moment and then explained that he would make a Trap with honey inside it so that Pooh would smell it and go after it.

And so, before Pooh became too lost in his
dreams of that sticky honey smell,
Piglet sent him to fetch some
honey while he set about
digging the deep pit.

Pooh went home to find only one pot of honey
left on his shelf. *Surely* he had some more?
Oh well, never mind.
This would have to do, he thought.

A little while later, Pooh returned with a honey pot. He passed it down to Piglet who was at the bottom of the pit.

"Is that all you had left?" Piglet said, peering into the jar. Pooh had to confess that he'd eaten some of the honey, just to make sure that it was honey and not anything else – cheese perhaps.

Piglet left the jar at the bottom of the Pit and the two friends said goodnight, agreeing to meet early the following morning to see how many heffalumps they had caught in the trap.

That night, Pooh woke up suddenly with a funny feeling in his tummy. He knew what that funny feeling meant – he was HUGNRY! So he went to the larder and reached up for a jar of honey. But he found NOTHING. Pooh was rather muddled and walked up and down, murmuring a murmur in a puzzled sort of way, before he remembered that he had put his last pot of honey into the Trap to catch a heffalump.

"Bother!" he said, and went back to bed.

But Pooh couldn't sleep and after trying **Counting Sheep**, he tried counting heffalumps.

But that was no good either. He jumped out of bed and ran straight to the spot where the Very Deep Pit had been dug.

There, at the bottom, was his jar of honey. And although he had already eaten most of it there was a little left at the very bottom of the jar.

He pushed his head into the jar and began to lick . . .

Meanwhile, Piglet woke up, his mind still a bit of a whirl with heffalump wonderings. Like . . .

"What if heffalumps didn't like pigs very much?" and other such worrying thoughts.

He comforted himself with the knowledge that Pooh would be with him, but perhaps heffalumps didn't like Bears either . . .

He decided to be brave and check the Trap for heffalumps. Off he went, muttering "Oh, dear, oh, dear, oh, dear!" as he did so. When he reached the trap, he peered in.

At that moment, **a loud roaring noise** arose from the Pit and Piglet, as frightened as a little pig can be, scampered away.

"Help, help!" he cried. "A Herrible Hoffalump! *Help!* A Hoffable Hellerump!" And he didn't stop until he got to Christopher Robin's house.

"Whatever's the matter, Piglet?" asked Christopher Robin. Piglet explained about the heffalump and how it had the biggest head you ever saw, like an enormous jar . . .

Christopher Robin agreed to come and look at it. He, too, could hear something as they got near the Pit. Then he began to laugh. And he laughed and laughed and laughed . . .

The terrible noise was Pooh,

with his head stuck in the jar,

BANGING

against a tree-root.

At that moment, his head popped out, and, on seeing Pooh Bear (not a heffalump), Piglet realised what a silly animal he'd been.

He felt so very silly that he ran straight home to bed with a headache, while Christopher Robin and Pooh shared a loving chuckle before setting off to have breakfast together.

Not long after Piglet's adventure with the **heffalump Trap,** the Hundred Acre Wood was a very wet place to be, for it rained and rained and rained.

One morning, little Piglet looked out of his window and wished that he'd had Company all this time, for then at least he might have had a jolly time talking with Pooh or Christopher Robin about it. After all, it was quite exciting to see such a flood. But Piglet did feel a little Anxious.

"Pooh could escape by Climbing Trees," he thought, "Kanga could Jump, Owl could fly . . . and here am I surrounded by water and I can't do anything."

Still it rained and rained, and every day the water got higher, until it was nearly up to Piglet's window. It was at this point that Piglet decided he should do something, and he thought and thought of what that something might be. Then he remembered that Christopher Robin had told him a story about a man on a desert island who wrote a message in a bottle before throwing it into the sea. *That's* what he would do! Then perhaps someone might find the bottle and come to rescue him.

So he found a bottle and some paper and a pencil, then he wrote:

HELP!
PIGLIT (ME)

before putting the
paper in the bottle
and corking the bottle tightly.

He leaned out of the window as far as he could
without falling into the water and dropped the bottle
with a splash! Watching it bob away into the distance, he
hoped someone would find it very soon. Then he sighed
a long sigh and wished that his friend Pooh was there
because it was so very much more friendly with two.

Meanwhile, Pooh Bear woke up after a very long sleep to find his house was flooded and his feet were wet.

"This is Serious," he said to himself. And with that, he took his **biggest** pot of honey and escaped with it to a large branch of his tree.

Then he climbed down to get the next pot of honey, and the next one after that, and the next one after that . . . until his Escape was complete and Pooh was sitting on the branch with ten pots of honey beside him.

One by one, he ate them all and it was while
enjoying the last sticky mouthful of the last pot of
honey that he noticed Piglet's bottle floating past
him. With only one thing on his mind, he plunged
into the water with a loud cry of "Honey!"

But it soon became clear no honey was inside.
"Bother!" said Pooh. Then he saw
the piece of paper. He took it out and pondered

upon it for a moment.

"Hmmm," he said. "It's a
Missage. That's what it is
. . . and that letter is
a 'P' and 'P' means
'Pooh'." He decided to
find Christopher Robin
or Owl to help him read it.

Being a Bear who couldn't swim, Pooh realised he would have to find another way to get to them. An idea came to him, one he was rather pleased about (being a Bear of Very Little Brain):

"If a bottle can float," he said to himself, "a jar can float, and if it's a big enough jar, I can sit on top of it."

So he took his biggest jar and made it watertight. Naming his new found vessel *The Floating Bear,* he set off, bobbing up and down a bit, just managing to paddle through the rainwater.

It was just about this moment in time, that in
another part of the Wood, Christopher Robin
bumped into Owl. Together they were wondering
whether Pooh and Piglet were all right in these rainy
conditions and just as Christopher Robin began to
worry about his lovable Bear, a growly voice behind
him said,

"Hello, I'm here!"

Christopher Robin was so pleased to see Pooh that he gave him a huge hug.

Pooh proudly showed him his boat and then the **Very Important Message** in the bottle.

"It's from Piglet!" cried Christopher Robin, reading the message (it was then that Pooh realised the "Ps" were for "Piglet" and not for "Pooh").

"We must rescue him!" said Pooh.

With that, he sent Owl off to tell Piglet that Rescue was on its way.

By now, Piglet was beginning to think that perhaps he might *never* be rescued and that he would try hard to be very brave.

So he was most grateful to see Owl, when he arrived to tell him of the coming Rescue, although the Rescue didn't come soon enough for poor Piglet, who had to listen to Owl's very long story about an aunt who laid a seagull's egg by mistake.

Feeling very tired, Piglet began to fall asleep and it was only a loud

SQUAWK!

from Owl that woke him with a start and stopped him falling out of the window into the water.

You can therefore imagine his joy and relief when he saw Christopher Robin and Pooh floating towards him in an *umbrella!* (Pooh had astounded even Christopher Robin with his clever umbrella idea).

At last, he was being rescued! Once again, he could be with his *dearest* friend, Pooh Bear and enjoy some Company.

And that is the end of Piglet's Big Adventure in the rain – an adventure in which, I think you'll agree, he was a Very Brave Piglet.